THE COMPLETE CHANSONS
Livre second des chansons . . . (1590)

RECENT RESEARCHES IN THE MUSIC OF THE RENAISSANCE

James Haar and Howard Mayer Brown, general editors

A-R Editions, Inc., publishes six quarterly series—

Recent Researches in the Music of the Middle Ages and Early Renaissance,
Margaret Bent, general editor;

Recent Researches in the Music of the Renaissance,
James Haar and Howard Mayer Brown, general editors;

Recent Researches in the Music of the Baroque Era,
Robert L. Marshall, general editor;

Recent Researches in the Music of the Classical Era,
Eugene K. Wolf, general editor;

Recent Researches in the Music of the Nineteenth and Early Twentieth Centuries,
Rufus Hallmark, general editor;

Recent Researches in American Music,
H. Wiley Hitchcock, general editor—

which make public music that is being brought to light
in the course of current musicological research.

Each volume in the *Recent Researches* is devoted
to works by a single composer or to a single genre of composition,
chosen because of its potential interest to scholars and performers,
and prepared for publication according to the standards that govern
the making of all reliable historical editions.

Subscribers to this series, as well as patrons of subscribing institutions,
are invited to apply for information about the "Copyright-Sharing Policy"
of A-R Editions, Inc., under which the contents of this volume
may be reproduced free of charge for study or performance.

Correspondence should be addressed:

A-R EDITIONS, INC.
315 West Gorham Street
Madison, Wisconsin 53703

RECENT RESEARCHES IN THE MUSIC OF THE RENAISSANCE • VOLUME LXI

André Pevernage

THE COMPLETE CHANSONS

Livre second
des chansons . . . (1590)

Edited by Gerald R. Hoekstra

A-R EDITIONS, INC. • MADISON

ANDRE PEVERNAGE
THE COMPLETE CHANSONS
Edited by Gerald R. Hoekstra

Recent Researches in the Music of the Renaissance

Library of Congress Cataloging in Publication Data:

Pevernage, André, 1542 or 3–1591.
   [Chansons, livre 2nd]
   Livre second des chansons—(1590)

   (The complete chansons / André Pevernage ; [v. 2])

   (Recent researches in the music of the Renaissance,
ISSN 0486-123X ; v. 61)
   For superius, quinta, contratenor, tenor, and bassus.
   French words.
   Edited from the 1st ed. published: Antwerp :
C. Plantin, 1590.
   Words also printed as text with English transla-
tions: p.
   Includes bibliographical references.
   1. Chansons, Polyphonic.   I. Hoekstra, Gerald R.
II. Series: Pevernage, André, 1542 or 3–1591.   Chansons ;
v. 2.   III. Series: Recent researches in the music of
the Renaissance ; v. 61.
M2.R2384   vol. 61   [M1582]   83-9963
ISBN 0-89579-183-8 (set)
ISBN 0-89579-188-9 (v. 2)

Contents

Introduction

Livre second des chansons . . . (1590)

Four books of André Pevernage's chansons were published between 1589 and 1591, and four other chansons by Pevernage were included in anthologies published in 1590 and 1597. All of Pevernage's chansons are edited in the present RECENT RESEARCHES IN THE MUSIC OF THE RENAISSANCE series (in RRRen volumes LX–LXIV). This volume includes all of the music of Pevernage's *Livre second des chansons*, and this Introduction deals specifically with that source. For information of a more general nature concerning the composer and his music, see the Preface in RRRen volume LX.[1]

The Antwerp publishing house of Christopher Plantin released André Pevernage's *Livre second des chansons* in the spring of 1590, just a few months after the *Chansons . . . Livre premier* and less than a year before the set was completed with the *Livre troisième* and the *Livre quatrième*. The dedications of Pevernage's four books of chansons, respectively, bear the dates 6 October 1589; 1 March 1590; 15 June 1590; and 12 January 1591. Assembling and printing these chanson books was only one of a number of projects on which Pevernage and Plantin had collaborated: the composer served as musical adviser to the publishing firm while he was *maistre de la chapelle* at the Cathedral of Notre Dame in Antwerp, a post he had held since 1585. It is possible that he served in this capacity even before 1585, since he had resided in Antwerp after fleeing the Protestants' invasion of Courtrai in 1578.[2] The Pevernage chanson books constituted one of the last projects for both men, however; Plantin died in 1589 before Book I was released, and Pevernage died on 30 July 1591, less than seven months after the completion of the set.

Like the earlier volume, *Livre second des chansons d'André Pevernage* was printed in five partbooks that bear the voice designations Superius, Contratenor, Tenor, Bassus, and Quinta. Plate I is a reproduction of the title page from the Superius partbook. Complete copies of the set of partbooks are held by the Bayerische Staatsbibliothek, Munich, and by the Österreichische Nationalbibliothek, Vienna; copies of the Superius, Contratenor, and Bassus books can also be found in the collection of the Gemeentemuseum, The Hague.

In the formal and obsequious vocabulary typical of the period, Pevernage dedicated his *Livre second des chansons* to Frederic de Granvelle-Perrenot, "Chevalier, Baron de Renaix, d'Aspremont, Seigneur de Beaujeu, St. Loup, Champagney, etc., Chef des Finances du Roy, & Gouverneur pour sa Mté. des Ville, Cité, territoire, & Marquisat d'Anvers" (see Plate II):

> My Lord, because the singular affection that your Illustrious Lordship has always borne toward Music has been acknowledged and experienced by me for a long time, and hoping to do nothing disagreeable to that by offering to you some little fruit of my harvest, I have made bold to present you with these my entertaining Chansons; beseeching very humbly that you take note not so much of the smallness of the gift as the good will of the giver: who of a truth wishes for nothing more than to be able, as much as lies in his power, to be of some service to your I[llustrious] L[ordship]. Thus, I present to you, My Lord, this, my little book, in order that it may more surely be brought to light under your protection and safeguard; trusting for that which I dare not hope—either by its own merit or that of its Author—that it may obtain this by the favor of your Illustrious Lordship; I hope for similar favor of many others; I do not doubt that they will favor it all the more when they see that it is dedicated to such a good and excellent patron. Meanwhile, I pray the Almighty, My Lord, to keep you always in his holy protection; commending myself very humbly to the good graces of Your I[llustrious] L[ordship]. Antwerp, this 1st of March, 1590.
>
> Your very humble and affectionate servant,
> André Pevernage.

Frederic de Granvelle-Perrenot was a brother of Antoine Perrenot, Cardinal Granvelle, who had figured so prominently in the government of Phillip II during the 1570s and 1580s.

The *Livre second* contains twenty-eight pieces—twenty-four if the constituent pieces of *pièces liées* are counted as single chansons.[3] Like those of Books I and III, all the chansons are for five voices. Unlike Book I, which is devoted to *chansons spirituelles*, Book II consists entirely of *chansons profanes*.

It is the only one of the four books that contains no motets; all of the pieces have French texts.

The chansons of Book II are grouped by mode as follows:

nos. 1–4	Hypodorian on D
nos. 5–7	Hypoionian on C
nos. 8–9	Aeolian on A
nos. 10–14	Dorian on G
nos. 15–17	Ionian on F
nos. 18–19	Phrygian on A
nos. 20–24	Hypodorian on G
nos. 25–28	Hypoionian on F

Thus, nos. 1–9 have no flat in the key signature; nos. 10–28 have a B-flat. The distinction between authentic and plagal modes appears in a comparison of ranges: voice parts in the plagal modes generally lie a fourth below their counterparts in the authentic modes. As in the other three chanson volumes issued by Plantin, the Dorian and Ionian modes and their plagal counterparts predominate.

her innocence by taking her own life.[4] The second *dizain* (set in no. 21) is the poet's paean of praise to this virtuous woman and her noble resolve. In the content of the story—though not in musical style—the chanson strongly resembles the two moralistic narratives set in Book I, *Joseph requis de femme mariée* (RRRen vol. LX, nos. 11–12) and *Susann' un jour* (RRRen vol. LX, no. 13), the Protestant poem so popular among sixteenth-century composers. In *Lucrec' un jour par force violée*, the phrase, "de toy, Tarquin" ("by you, Tarquin") suggests that the chanson may have been part of a theatrical production (see mm. 7–10).

Of the poets whose texts are set in the chansons, Clément Marot predominates. His name is associated with seven chansons of Book II—fully a fourth of the pieces in the volume. Other texts are by Philippe Desportes, Pierre de Ronsard, and Mellin de St.-Gelais. Table 1 cites all of the known poets of Pevernage's Book II and designates, as well, the poetic form or genre of the texts.[5]

Table 1

CHANSON	TITLE	POET	FORM OR GENRE
Nos. 1–3	Fay que je vive	Desportes	*baiser*
No. 4	Scavez vous	Desportes	*chanson*
Nos. 6–7	Ton gentil coeur	Marot	*élégie*
No. 8	Là me tiendray	Marot	*rondeau*
No. 9	Je suis tellement	Ronsard	*chanson*
No. 13	D'estr' amoureux	Marot	*rondeau*
No. 14	Secouré moy	Marot	*chanson*
No. 16	Toutes les nuicts	Marot	*rondeau*
No. 22	Tant seulement	Marot	*rondeau*
No. 28	De moins que Rien	St.-Gelais	*huitain*

As one would expect, the texts of most of the chansons of Book II deal with love. They lament the plight of the lover, decry the inconstancy of love, or laud the virtues and beauty of the loved one. The few texts that do not touch these love themes directly nevertheless deal with them implicitly. One of these, *Triste fortune au bas m'a voulu attirer* (no. 19), praises constancy in general, although the poet probably had constancy in love in mind. Another chanson, *De moins que Rien* (no. 28), has as its text a clever piece of verse that deals with the theme of contentment; this text might apply to love as well as to any other area of life. The remaining chanson with a subject other than love, per se, is the *pièce liée*, *Lucrec' un jour par force violée* (nos. 20–21). In the first *dizain* of this anonymous poem, Lucretia (a noblewoman of ancient Rome) recounts the sad tale of her rape by Tarquin and swears her resolve to prove

The remaining poems, whose authorship is unknown, are, with one exception, essentially *chansons* of four, six, or eight lines. The possibility exists, of course, that some of these have been extracted from larger poems. The one anonymous poem with an identifiable form is no. 26, *Contente vous d'avoir tel serviteur*, which is a *rondeau*.

Except for the *rondeau*, none of the text genres cited in Table 1 denotes a specific form. The *chanson*, of course, is free in form and is light and rhythmic in character; as a genre, its distinctiveness stems not from its form or subject matter, but, as C. A. Mayer writes of Marot's *chansons*, from "le ton populaire, le simplicité de parfaite aisance" ("the popular tone, the simplicity of complete naturalness").[6] Marot's *Secouré moy ma dame par amours* (set in no. 14 of Book II) was one of the most popular *chansons* among composers of Pevernage's time: there are at least eight other settings of the poem, including compositions by di Lasso, Sermisy, de Monte, and Gombert.[7] "Baiser" does not seem to be a commonly used term for a poetic genre; but Desportes himself applies this designation to *Fay que je vive, ô ma seulle deesse* (set in nos. 1–3 of Book II) in his *Diverses amours*.[8] Like Marot's *élégie Ton gentil coeur si hautement assis*, of which Pevernage set (in nos. 6–7) only selected lines,[9] it resembles the *chansons* in style and spirit.

Likewise, the *rondeaux* of Marot, even though they follow stylized forms, exhibit the lightness and freedom that characterize the *chanson*. The *rondeau* was, of course, one of the *formes fixes* used by poets for several centuries. It was already considered old-fashioned by Marot's time, and, in fact, almost all of Marot's sixty-four *rondeaux* are products of his youth and were published in his *L'Adolescence clémentine* (1532).[10] The form used by Marot was the *rondeau double* (*a a b b a, a a b* R, *a a b b a* R), in which the first five lines are repeated as the refrain. Pevernage, like other sixteenth-century composers, set only the refrain.

The musical forms and styles of the chansons in this volume are characteristic of Pevernage's chansons in general in that the settings are tied closely to their texts. Stylistic continuity unifies all repetitions of a phrase of text; contrast distinguishes settings of successive phrases. Repetition occurs, for the most part, only on this small, immediate scale. In the few instances where there are larger repeats, most notably at the end of the *pièces liées*, the repetition of the concluding section contributes to the sense of termination or conclusion. For example, in *Fay que mon am' à la tienne s'assemble* (no. 3), the third *partie* of *Fay que je vive, ô ma seulle deesse*, the two concluding lines of the six-line strophe are set initially in measures 11–21 and then repeated with the same musical setting in measures 21–29. The scale of this conclusion—involving two-thirds of the piece—indicates that it is clearly designed to function architecturally as the closing unit for the entire composition in three *parties*, not just for the one in which it appears. As a further means of unifying these three pieces, Pevernage drew on the same musical material for the opening phrase of text in the first two *parties*, although he diminished the rhythmic values for the second appearance. Sectional repetition also occurs at the end of *Lucrec' un jour par force violée* (nos. 20–21), *Je suis tellement amoureux* (no. 9), and *Si mon coeur a faict offence* (no. 18). The last of these is both unusual and puzzling because of the changes of rhythm that occur in the repetition. Measures 23–31 are repeated in measures 32–41, but with triple rather than duple rhythms.[11]

Pevernage's concern for textual rhythms and meanings varies greatly from piece to piece. In setting the more colorful or dramatic texts, such as *Triste fortune au bas m'a voulu attirer* (no. 19) and *Lucrec' un jour par force violée* (nos. 20–21), he wrote what are essentially madrigals with French texts. In most cases, however, even though the text elicits no particular musical imagery, the composer still treated each line with a setting appropriate to its rhythm and expression.

Editorial Commentary

This edition of the *Livre second des chansons . . .* (1590) is based on the complete set of partbooks in the Bayerische Staatsbibliothek of Munich (shelf number Mus pr 32/1), which was made available to the editor on microfilm. Except for the shadows caused by some bleeding through of the ink on a number of pages, the source is clear and easy to read. Brackets enclose editorial additions and alterations. However, although titles have been added by the editor, they are not bracketed.[12] The barlines drawn through the staves are also editorial. Horizontal brackets (⌐¬) mark notes that appear as ligatures in the source.

No problems with text underlay were encountered, because Pevernage's style is predominantly syllabic, and because Plantin took great care for the accuracy of text placement in his publications. In the source, all repetitions of text are either written out or indicated with the sign *ij*. No additional editorial repetitions were necessary.

For the most part, spelling and punctuation of the texts remain unaltered. However, all abbreviations, including ampersands, have been written out, and archaic spellings with "u," "v," and "i" have been changed to their modern forms whenever the original version might confuse the reader, as, for instance, in *ie viue* (*je vive*). The use of contractions and apostrophes to indicate elisions follows the source. Accents have been added to vowels where they were omitted from the source (either by mistake or because the practice was not standard) and where their absence might affect pronunciation or confuse the reader. Spellings have otherwise not been modernized, even though it is thought that the pronunciation, with a few exceptions, should not differ substantially from modern forms of the same words. The most frequently encountered archaism is the obsolete "s," which would not have been pronounced.[13] In this edition, syllable divisions indicate whether the "s" is to be pronounced or not; where the "s" falls before the division, it is silent; where it falls after the division, it must be pronounced. For example, in *mais-tre* and *vos-tre* the "s" is silent; in *tri-stesse* and *e-sprits*, the "s" is pronounced. Another common archaism is seen in spellings with "oi," where modern French has "ai," as in *regnoit* (*regnait*), *resistoit* (*resistait*), or *apparoistre* (*apparaître*). Again, the modern "ai" sound should be used.

Punctuation follows the source for the most part, but some editorial changes were made for the sake of clarity. In many cases, the punctuation following a phrase of text in the source is not clear because the final appearance of the phrase is indicated with the *ij* sign, and thus includes no punctuation. Full stops (usually indicated in the edition with a colon) were added where the comma used in the source seemed insufficient, or where a colon was lacking in the source because the phrase of text makes its last appearance by means of a repeat sign.

The editorial incipit of the music gives the name, clef, key signature, mensuration sign, and first note of each part as found in Plantin's print. For the G- and moveable C- and F-clefs of the source, this edition uses the treble, tenor G-clef, and bass clef. Although its name has been retained, the placement of the Quinta voice varies from piece to piece, depending on its range. Where the range of the Quinta corresponds to that of the Superius, it is placed on the fourth staff line from the bottom. Where its range is that of the Tenor, it appears on the middle staff. Ranges of all voices are indicated immediately before the modern clefs. (Performers should note that the range does not always give a reliable impression of the tessitura; for instance, the bottom note of the specified range may appear only once or twice in certain works, and the most common low note in the piece may otherwise be a fourth above that indicated in the range-finder.

Note values in this edition have been reduced by half, except for the final note of each piece, which is a longa in the source and has been transcribed here as a whole-note with a fermata. Pevernage used only two mensuration signs, ¢ and C, but with no apparent distinction in musical styles or rhythmic values. It is probable that Pevernage, like many of his contemporaries, did not intend different meanings for the two signs; but they have nonetheless been retained.

Accidentals that appear within the staff are original; those that appear above the staff are editorial and include both cautionary accidentals and *musica ficta*. Editorial accidentals have been supplied sparingly, and consideration has been given to general sixteenth-century practices as well as to Pevernage's own idiosyncracies. Where sharp signs in the source cancel flats, they have been changed to naturals in the edition. In the source an accidental is valid only for successive notes of the same pitch, unless the second statement of that pitch begins a new phrase, in which case the validity of the accidental is not always clear. In the source, an accidental is canceled either by a rest or by an intervening note of a different pitch, and this system is also followed here, since it seems clearest in music with such frequent and temporary pitch alterations. Thus, accidentals that are redundant in modern practice are, nevertheless, preserved here. Both original and editorial accidentals should be considered valid for consecutive notes within measures. In a given voice, where previously inflected pitches recur after intervening notes and the accidental must be invalidated, an editorial reminder is provided above the staff.

The shape of the melodic lines in many places may tempt the reader to raise or lower pitches in accordance with the rules of *musica ficta*. However, performers must be careful to take note of the other voices: such alterations will often result in cross-relations within a chord or in augmented harmonies. The extreme care, frequency, and consistency with which Pevernage supplied accidentals make it doubtful that he intended the performer to add many of his own. A notable departure from normal sixteenth-century practice in this respect is his avoidance of diminished harmonies in the first inversion for penultimate chords at cadences (i.e., dim. VII⁶–I). Although he invariably supplied a sharp to the third where the penultimate chord lies a fourth below the cadence chord, and where anyone familiar with the style would add one anyway, he consistently left unaltered those penultimate chords that have their roots a major second below the cadence chord and in which the cadence is approached by 2–1 motion in the lowest voice.[14] Pevernage's consistency in this matter suggests that he intended the VII⁶ to remain unaltered.

Coloration appears only in no. 18, where it has been enclosed in broken horizontal brackets (⌐ ¬) and transcribed as triplets. The combination of a colored semibreve and minim (◆ ♩) often served in the sixteenth century as an alternate way of notating the dotted rhythm ♩· ♪, usually notated by a dotted minim and a semiminim. However, this way of notating the dotted rhythm does not occur anywhere else in the four Pevernage chanson books issued by Plantin, and thus it is extremely doubtful that Pevernage intended dotted rhythms here. Furthermore, the triplet feeling of measures 23ff., which have the same text and harmonies, confirms the conclusion that the composer intended triplets.

Critical Notes

The following list notes errors in the source, accidentals made superfluous by the editorial procedure, and other discrepancies, all of which are minor, between the present edition and the source. Pitches are designated according to the usual system, wherein middle C is c', the C above middle C is c'', and so forth.

No. 3—Mm. 1–3, Tenor and Bassus, the first phrase of text is printed without notes at this point in the source. M. 20, Contratenor, note 4 is g'-sharp in the source, resulting in a melodic augmented second.

No. 6—M. 56, Quinta, note 3 is a semiminim in the source.

No. 11—Mm. 17–19, all parts, underlaid text reads: "Autant que puis treshumblement"; word "puis" changed to "suis" here in order to make proper sense in this phrase.

No. 16—M. 10, Contratenor, note 4 is a dotted semibreve in the source.

No. 19—M. 21, Superius, note 2 has a cautionary sharp in the source.

No. 20—M. 18, Contratenor, note 6 has a cautionary sharp in the source.

No. 21—Mm. 1–3, Tenor and Bassus, the incipit of text "O coeur hautain" is printed without notes at this point in the source.

No. 22—M. 29, Quinta, note 4 has a sharp in the source; this is apparently a mistake, since a conflict results with note 4 in the Tenor.

No. 24—M. 10, Contratenor, notes 2–3, the internal b-flat to c'-sharp has been retained here, even though an augmented second results. For a similar instance, cf. no. 3, m. 20, Contratenor, where it seemed less acceptable and was therefore altered.

No. 25—Mm. 33–37, all parts, underlaid text "cachez" is retained here from the source; it should probably be "caches."

No. 28—Mm. 1–5, Bassus, the first line of text is printed without notes at this point in the source.

Notes

1. Books I, II, and III (RRRen vols. LX–LXII) all contain chansons *a 5*; Book IV (RRRen vols. LXIII–LXIV) consists of chansons *a 6, 7,* and *8.* The four chansons from other collections—three chansons *a 4* and a chanson *a 2* in three *parties*—are included at the end of RRRen vol. LXIV. For further information on the composer, his chanson publications, and his musical style, the reader is directed to the more substantial Preface in RRRen vol. LX and to Gerald R. Hoekstra, "The Chansons of André Pevernage (1542/43–1591)" (Ph.D. diss., The Ohio State University, 1975).

2. For a biographical study of Pevernage, see J.-A Stellfeld, *Andries Pevernage: zijn leven—zijne werken* (Louvain: De vlaamsche Drukkerij, N.V., 1943).

3. *Pièces liées,* sets of two or more pieces intended to be sung together, are, in a sense, single multipartite units, and therefore when they are referred to in the Introduction and Notes, their numbers will be joined with an N-dash (e.g., nos. 6–7).

4. The Roman historian Livy recounts the story of Lucretia. See Livy, *Book I,* ch. 58.

5. The two poems by Desportes come, respectively, from his *Diverses amours* (1573) and *Les amours d'Hippolyte* (1573); see the modern editions by Victor E. Graham, *Diverses amours et autres oeuvres mellées* (Geneva: Librairie Droz, 1963) and *Les amours d'Hippolyte* (Geneva: Librairie Droz, 1960). The Ronsard *chanson* comes from his *Amours* (1587), the source of numerous sixteenth-century song texts. For a modern edition of the *Amours,* see *Les oeuvres de Pierre de Ronsard: texte de 1587,* ed. Isadore Silver (Chicago: The University of Chicago Press, 1966). Marot's *Ton gentil coeur si hautement assis* is numbered in the standard editions of his works as *Elégie XV*; *Secouré moy ma dame par amours* is his *Chanson II*; and the four *rondeaux* in order of their appearance in Pevernage's volume are *Rondeaux XLV, IX, XLIII,* and *LII*—see C. A. Mayer's editions, *Clément Marot: Oeuvres lyriques* (London: University of London, The Athlone Press, 1964) and *Oeuvres diverses: rondeaux, ballades, chants royaux, epitaphes, etrennes, sonnets* (London: University of London, Athlone Press, 1966), p. 7.

6. C. A. Mayer, ed., *Clément Marot: Oeuvres lyriques,* p. 12.

7. François Lesure, "Autour de Clément Marot et de ses musiciens," *Revue de musicologie* 33 (1951): 118–119.

8. See Philippe Desportes, *Diverses amours et autres oeuvres mellées,* p. 193.

9. Pevernage set lines 1–6 and 9–10 in his *premiére partie* (no. 6) and lines 11–14 in his *seconde partie* (no. 7).

10. C. A. Mayer, ed., *Oeuvres diverses: rondeaux, ballades, chants royaux, epitaphes, etrennes, sonnets,* p. 7.

11. See the Editorial Commentary for a brief discussion of this notation.

12. Although Plantin's publication does not bear titles at the tops of the pages of music, it does furnish them in a list of contents at the rear of the volume. Pevernage's titles usually consist of the first three or four words of the text. Longer ti-

tles have been furnished for this edition, since one occasionally encounters sixteenth-century poems that begin with the same incipit but are otherwise quite different.

13. An excellent source of information on pronunciation is Jeannine Alton and Brian Jeffery, *Bele Buche e Bele Parleure: A Guide to the Pronunciation of Medieval and Renaissance French for Singers and Others* (London: Tecla Editions, 1976). Further information may be found in E.-J. Bourciez, *Phonétique française* (Paris: Editions Klinksieck, n.d.).

14. In only two places in this volume have I been able to find cadences with a diminished penultimate chord. In one of these, it occurs without an accidental (no. 8, mm. 33–34) and in the other with a raised F (no. 21, m. 27). For instances in which it seems appropriate to raise the degree that moves up to the root of the cadence chord, but for which the composer has not supplied an accidental, the reader is referred to the following: no. 4, m. 20 (Tenor), m. 22 (Contratenor), m. 27 (Quinta); no. 6, m. 33 (Quinta); and no. 16, m. 29 (Superius).

Texts and Translations

The following translations from the French were made by the editor with the helpful advice and guidance of Dr. William Huseman. They are literal rather than poetic translations.

Livre second des chansons . . . (1590)

No. 1   [1. partie]   Philippe Desportes

Fay que je vive, ô ma seulle deesse!
Fay que je vive, et change ma tristesse
   En plaisir gracieux:
Change ma mort en immortelle vie,
Et fay mon coeur que mon ame ravie
   S'envoll' entre les dieux.

(Let me live, o my only goddess,
Le me live, and change my sadness
   Into carefree pleasure.
Change my death into immortal life,
And change my heart so that my enraptured soul
   May take flight among the gods.)

No. 2   2. partie

Fay que je vive, et fay qu'à la mesm' heure
Baissant les yeux, entre tes bras je meure,
   Languissant doucement:
Puis qu' aussitost doucement je revive,
Pour amortir la flamm' ardent et vive,
   Qui me va consumant.

(Let me live, and while
I am closing my eyes, let me die in your arms,
   Languishing sweetly.
Then at once let me sweetly come to life again
In order to extinguish the ardent flame of love
   That is consuming me.)

No. 3   3. partie

Fay que mon am' à la tienne s'assemble,
Range nos coeurs et nos esprits ensemble
   Sous une mesme loy:
Qu'à mon desir ton desir se rapporte;
Vy dedans moy, et en la mesme sorte,
   Je vivray dedans toy.

(Let my soul and yours come together,
Arrange our hearts and our spirits together
   Under the same rule;
That your desire may agree with mine.
Live within me, and in the same way
   I will live within you.)

No. 4   Philippe Desportes

Scavez vous ce que je desire
Pour loyer de ma fermeté?
Que vous puissiez voir mon martyre,
Comme je voy vostre beauté.

(Do you know what I desire
As the reward for my firmness?
That you be able to see my torment
As I see your beauty.)

No. 5

Vous qui goutez d'amour le doux contentement,
Chantez qu'il n'est rien tel que l'estat d'un amant:
Vous qui la liberté pour deess' avez prize,
Chantez qu'il n'est rien tel que garder sa franchise.

(You who taste the sweet contentment of love,
Sing that there is nothing quite like the state of a
   lover.
You who have taken liberty as a goddess,
Sing that there is nothing quite like keeping your
   freedom.)

No. 6   [1. partie]   Clément Marot

Ton gentil coeur si hautement assis,
Ton sens discret à merveille rassis,
Ton noble port, ton maintien asseuré,
Ton chant si doux, ton parler mesuré,
Ton propr' habit, qui tant bien se conforme
Au naturel de ta tresbelle forme,
Ne m'ont induict à t'offrir le service
De mon las coeur plein d'amour sans malice.

(Your noble heart, so highly placed,
Your discreet and marvelously calm way,
Your noble carriage, your assured manner,

Your song so sweet, your measured speech,
Your proper dress, which conforms so naturally
To the lines of your beautiful form,
Are not what led me to offer you the service
Of my weary heart, full of love, without ill intent.)

No. 7   *2. partie*

Ce fut pour vray le doux traict de tes yeux,
Et de ta bouch' aucuns mots gracieux,
Qui de bien loing me viendrent fair' entendre,
Secretement, qu'a m'aymer voulois tendre.

(It was, truly, the sweet arrow of your eyes,
And from your mouth a few gracious words
That from afar led me to understand
That, secretly, you wished to reach out to love me.)

No. 8   Clément Marot

Là me tiendray où à present me tien:
Car ma maistresse au plaisant entretien
M'ayme d'un coeur tant bon et desirable,
Qu'on me devroit appeller miserable
Si mon vouloir estoit autre que sien.

(There will I stay where I already am;
For my mistress, with pleasant demeanor,
Loves me with a heart so good and desirable
That one would have to call me despicable
If my desire were other than hers.)

No. 9   Pierre de Ronsard

Je suis tellement amoureux,
Qu'au vray raconter je ne puis
Ny où je suis, ne que je suis,
Ny combien je suis malheureux.

(I am so much in love
That truly I cannot tell you
Where I am, nor what I am,
Nor how unhappy I am.)

No. 10

Amour vrayment est une maladie,
Les medecins la sçavent bien juger
En la nommant fureur de fantasie,
Qui ne se peut par herbes soulager.

(Truly love is a sickness;
The doctors know how to judge it
In calling it the fury of fantasy
That cannot be relieved by herbs.)

No. 11

Si mon devoir ne fay ma dame
De vous traicter royalement,
Je vous prie ne m'en donner blame,
Autant que suis treshumblement,
Vostre subject humainement.
Festoyons les de toute part,
Chantons, buvons joyeusement,
Ne le prenez de malapart.

(If I do not do my duty, my lady,
In my efforts to treat you royally,
I pray that you will not blame me for it,
Especially since I am most humbly
And courteously your subject.
Let us fête everywhere,
Let us sing and drink joyously;
Do not be offended.)

No. 12

Certes vous avez tort, et ne scaurois penser
Que Dieu peust un tel faict en silence passer:
N'estimez toutesfois, quoy que vous pensiez faire
Que de vostr' amitié je me puisse distraire.

(Certainly you are wrong, and [I] could not conceive
That God can pass over such a deed in silence:
However, whatever you might think of doing, do
    not imagine
That I could be prevented from seeking your
    affection.)

No. 13   Clément Marot

D'estr' amoureux n'ay plus intention:
C'est maintenant ma moindr' affection,
Car celle là de qui je cuidois estre
Le bien aymé m'a bien faict apparoistre
Qu'au faict d'amour n'y a que fiction.

(Being in love is no more my aspiration;
It is now my least desire,
For one of whom I thought I was the beloved
Has made clear to me
That, as far as love is concerned, there is only
    pretense.)

No. 14   Clément Marot

Secouré moy ma dame par amours,
Ou autrement la mort me vient querir.
Autre que vous ne peut donner secours
A mon las coeur, lequel s'en va mourir.
Helas, Helas, vueillez doncq secourir

Celuy qui vit pour vous en grand detresse,
Car de son coeur vous estes la maistresse.

(Succor me, my lady, with love,
Or else death will come to take me.
No one but you can give comfort
To my weary heart, which is about to die.
Alas, alas, then would you be so good as to succor
Him who lives for you in great distress,
For of his heart you are the mistress.)

No. 15

Si le souffrir donnoit espoir,
Combien seroit ma pein' heureuse,
Mais sans espoir tousjours douloir,
Je tiens qu'il n'est mort plus facheuse:
Tell' est la pein' et le tourment
Qui mon coeur tu' incessament.

(If suffering gave hope,
How happy would my pain be;
But I hold that there is no death worse
Than always being in sorrow without hope:
Such is the pain and torment
That kills my heart unceasingly.)

No. 16   Clément Marot

Toutes les nuicts je ne pense qu'en celle
Qui a le corps plus gent qu'une pucelle
De quatorz' ans, sur le point d'enrager,
Et au dedans un coeur, pour abbreger,
Autant joyeux qu'eut oncques damoiselle.

(Every night I think only of her
Who has a body more pleasing than a maiden
Of fourteen years—to the point of going mad—
And on the inside a heart, in short,
As joyous as ever a young woman had.)

No. 17

Le loyer de mon service,
Si rien ne puis de servir,
C'est que seulement servir
De vostre gré je vous puisse,
Et que m'ottroyez ce bien,
Puis qu'il ne vous couste rien.

(The reward for my service,
If I can do anything to serve you,
Is only to serve
You to your liking;
And that you might grant me this favor,
Since it will cost you nothing.)

No. 18

Si mon coeur a faict offence
De s'estr' à vous attaché,
Amour a faict le peché,
Et j'en fais la penitence:
Un peché selon les loix
Ne se doit punir deux fois.

(If my heart has committed an offense
By being attached to you,
It was love that prompted the sin,
And I am making penitence for it.
A sin, according to the law,
Must not be punished twice.)

No. 19

Triste fortune au bas m'a voulu attirer
Par ses havetz et du tout accabler,
Mais ses desseings n'a sceu effectuer.
Constanc' est bonne qui s'en peut emparer.

(Sad fortune wanted to pull me down
With its hooks and to overpower me completely,
But its designs could not be carried out;
Constancy is good for him who can take hold of it.)

No. 20   [1. partie]

Lucrec' un jour par force violée
De toy, Tarquin, fils du Roy orgueilleux,
A son baron (trist' et desconfortée)
Pleurant l'effort et faict outrageux,
Disoit: Helas! ce traistre convoiteux
De ce mien corps ravit la jouissance,
Mais mon esprit luy a fait resistence,
Tesmoin la mort, que sans aucun delay
(Pour esprouver à tous mon innocence)
En chastiant le corps je souffriray.

(Lucretia, forcibly violated one day
By you, Tarquin, son of the proud king,
Said to her husband (sad and discomforted),
Mourning the outrageous attempt and deed:
"Alas, the covetous traitor
Ravished my body for his pleasure,
But my spirit resisted him.
Witness the death that without delay
(To prove to all my innocence)
I will suffer to chasten this body.")

No. 21   2. partie

O coeur hautain, o courage pudique,
Que pour monstrer ta grande loyauté,

Choisis la mort, fuiant vie impudique,
Laissant exemple de ta chasteté:
Or maintenant si l'exquise beauté
De ton corps gent t'a mis à mort cruelle,
Ce non obstant ta memoir' eternelle
Ne cessera de vous nommer sans blame,
Noble Romaine Lucrece la belle,
Miroir de toute vertueuse dame.

(O lofty heart, o chaste courage,
That to show your great faithfulness
Chose death, fleeing unchaste life,
Leaving an example of your chastity.
Now, even though the exquisite beauty
Of your comely body caused your cruel death,
In spite of this, your eternal memory
Will continue to speak of you as blameless.
Noble Roman Lucretia the beautiful,
Mirror of every virtuous woman.)

No. 22   Clément Marot

Tant seulement ton amour je demande,
Te suppliant que ta beauté commande
Au coeur de moy comm' à ton serviteur,
Quoy que jamais il ne desservit heur,
Qui procedast d'une grace si grande.

(Only for your love I ask,
Begging you that your beauty might rule
This heart of mine as your servant,
Although it does not deserve the good fortune
That proceeds from such a great favor.)

No. 23

Puisqu'amour m'a voulu arrester
Pour vous servir, plaise vous me traiter
Comme voudries vous mesm' estre traitée,
Si vous esties par amour arrestée.

(Since love decided to retain me
In order to serve you, please treat me
As you would be treated
If you were arrested by love.)

No. 24

Si le Rubis par sa naive bonté,
Par son beau lustre et tresluissant couleur,
Tous coeurs humains rend de soy convoiteux,
Ce n'est merveille que vous qui en beauté
Le secondez en nom et en splendeur,
De ton amour me rends tant desireux.

(If the Ruby, by its simple goodness,
By its beautiful luster and sparkling color

Makes all human hearts covetous,
It is no wonder that you, who in your beauty
Second it in name and in splendor,
Make me so desirous of your love.)

No. 25

Chanson va-ten où je t'addresse,
Dans la chambre de ma maistresse:
Di luy, baisant sa blanche main,
Que pour en santé je remettre
Il ne luy faut, sinon permettre,
Que tu te cachez dans son sein.

(Chanson, go where I tell you to,
To the chamber of my mistress;
Tell her, kissing her white hand,
That in order to restore me to health
She need only allow
You to hide yourself in her bosom.)

No. 26

Contente vous d'avoir tel serviteur,
N'en cherchez pas au monde de meilleur,
Ayme le bien sans jamais l'etranger;
Car de sa part il ne vous veut changer,
Pour servir autre tant soit de grand' valeur.

(Be content with having such a servant,
Don't search the world for one better,
Love him well without ever betraying him;
As for his part, he would never exchange you
In order to serve another, even if she be of great
  worth.)

No. 27

Tout ce qui est au mond' est un jeu d'inconstance,
Et encor' en amour on voit moins d'asseurance:
Sa faveur est semblabl' à un beau jour d'hyver,
Qui se perd aussitost qu'on le voit arriver.

(Everything in the world is inconstant,
And especially in love one finds even less reliability:
Its favor is like a beautiful day in winter,
Which is lost as soon as one sees it arrive.)

No. 28   Mellin de St.-Gelais

De moins que Rien l'on peut à Peu venir:
Et puis ce Peu n'a si peu de puissance
Que bien ne fac' à Assez parvenir
Celuy qui veut aymer la suffisance.
Mais si à trop de malheur il s'avance,

Ne recevant d'Assez contentement,
En danger est par sa foll' inconstance
De retourner à son commencement.

(From less than Nothing one can come to a Little;
And then this Little does not have so little power
That he who wishes to enjoy contentment
Cannot make it come to Enough.
But if he has too much misfortune,
Not being content with Enough,
He puts himself in danger, by his foolish
  inconstancy,
Of returning to his beginning.)

LIVRE SECOND
DES CHANSONS
D'ANDRE PEVERNAGE,
MAISTRE DE LA CHAPELLE
DE L'EGLISE CATHEDRALE
D'ANVERS.

A cincq parties.

SVPERIVS.

A ANVERS,
De l'Imprimerie de Christofle Plantin.

M. D. XC.

Plate I. André Pevernage: *Livre second des chansons . . .* (1590)
Superius partbook, title page.
(Bayerische Staatsbibliothek, Munich)

A ILLVSTRE SEIGNEVR MESSIRE FREDRICQ DE GRANVELLE-PERRENOT,

CHEVALIER, BARON DE RENAIX, d'Aspremont, Seigneur de Beaujeu, St Loup, Champagney, &c. Chef des Finances du Roy, & Gouuerneur pour sa Mté des Ville, Cité, territoire, & Marquisat d'Anuers.

MONSEIGNEVR, d'autant que la singuliere affection que vostre Illustre Seigneurie tousiours a porté à la Musicque, m'a esté ia long temps notoire & experimentée, & esperant que ne feroy chose des-agreable à icelle, si ie luy offriroy quelque petit fruict de mon creu, i'ay prins la hardiesse de luy presenter ces miennes Chansons recreatifues; la suppliant treshumblemēt de n'auoir tant regard à la petitesse du don, qu'à la bonne volonté du donneur: qui à la verité rien plus ne souhaitte, que de pouuoir, en chose qui soit en sa puissance, faire quelque humble seruice à ladicte vostre I. S. Ie vous presente doncq, Monseigneur, ce mien liuret, à fin que plus seurement puisse soubs vostre protection & sauue-garde venir à la lumiere; me confiant que ce qu'il n'oseroyt esperer ny de soy ny de son Auteur, l'obtiendra par la faueur de vostre Illustre Seigneurie; i'entends pareille faueur de plusieurs autres, auxquels ie ne doute que d'autant plus il complaira, qu'ils voirront qu'il est dedié à vn si bon & excellent patron. Cependant ie prieray le Tout-puissant, MONSEIGNEVR, vous auoir tousiours en sa saincte garde; me recommandant treshumblement aux bonnes graces de V.I.S. D'Anuers ce 1. de Mars, M.D.XC.

Vostre treshumble & tresaffectionné seruiteur

André Peuernage.

Plate II. André Pevernage: *Livre second des chansons . . .* (1590)
Superius partbook, dedication page.
(Bayerische Staatsbibliothek, Munich)

Plate III. André Pevernage: *Livre second des chansons . . .* (1590)
Superius partbook, first page of *Fay que je vive, ô ma seulle deesse*, no. 1.
(Bayerische Staatsbibliothek, Munich)

LIVRE SECOND DES CHANSONS . . . (1590)

1. Fay que je vive, ô ma seule deesse

2. Fay que je vive, et fay qu'à la mesm' heure

[Philippe Desportes]

3. Fay que mon am' à la tienne s'assemble

8

4. Scavez vous ce que je desire

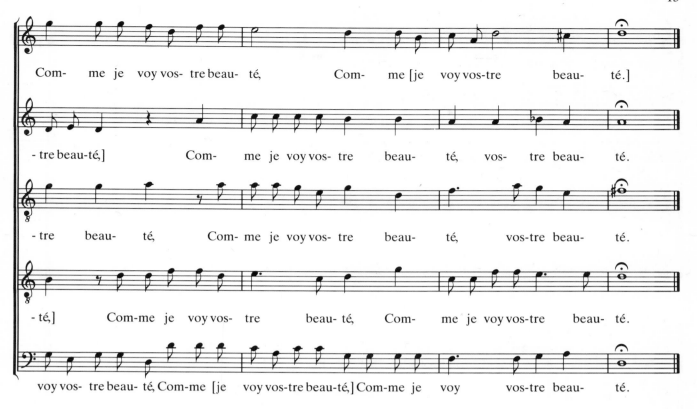

Com- me je voy vos- tre beau- té, Com- me [je voy vos-tre beau- té.]

- tre beau-té,] Com- me je voy vos- tre beau- té, vos- tre beau- té.

- tre beau- té, Com- me je voy vos- tre beau- té, vos-tre beau- té.

- té,] Com-me je voy vos- tre beau- té, Com- me je voy vos-tre beau- té.

voy vos- tre beau- té, Com-me [je voy vos-tre beau-té,] Com-me je voy vos-tre beau- té.

5. Vous qui goutez d'amour

Superius

Vous qui gou-tez d'a-mour le doux con-ten-te-ment, Vous qui gou-tez d'a-mour le doux con-

Quinta

Vous qui gou-tez d'a-mour le doux con-ten-te-ment,

Contratenor

Vous qui gou-tez d'a-mour le doux con-ten-te-ment, Vous [qui gou-tez d'a-mour le doux con-

Tenor

Vous qui gou-tez d'a-mour le doux con-

Bassus

Vous qui gou-tez d'a-mour le doux con-

14

16

6. Ton gentil coeur si hautement assis

18

7. Ce fut pour vray le doux traict

[Clément Marot]

Superius · 2. partie

Ce fut pour vray, [Ce fut pour vray,] Ce

Quinta

Ce fut pour vray, [Ce fut pour vray,] Ce fut pour vray, [Ce

Contratenor

Ce fut pour vray, [Ce fut pour vray,] Ce fut pour vray, [Ce

Tenor

Ce fut pour vray, [Ce fut pour vray]

Bassus

Ce fut pour vray, [Ce

fut _____ pour vray le doux traict de tes yeux, Et de ta

fut pour vray] le doux traict de tes yeux, le [doux traict de tes yeux,] Et de ta bou-

fut pour vray] le doux traict de tes yeux, le [doux traict de tes yeux,] Et de ta

le doux traict de tes yeux, Et de ta bou-

fut pour vray] le doux traict de tes yeux, Et de ta bou-

24

8. Là me tiendray où à present me tien

9. Je suis tellement amoureux

10. Amour vrayment est une maladie

11. Si mon devoir ne fay ma dame

38

12. Certes vous avez tort

13. D'estr' amoureux n'ay plus intention

14. Secouré moy ma dame par amours

-se, Car de son coeur, [Car de son coeur,] Car de son coeur, [Car de son

-se, Car de son coeur,_____ Car de son coeur,] Car de son

de son coeur, [Car de son coeur,] Car [de son

-se, Car de son coeur, [Car de son coeur]_____

-se, Car de son coeur, [Car de son

coeur, Car de son coeur] vous es- tes la mais-tres- se, [vous es- tes

coeur vous es- tes la mais- tres- se, vous [es- tes la mais-tres- se,] vous [es- tes

coeur] vous es- tes la mais-tres- se, vous [es- tes la mais-tres- se,] vous es- tes

vous es- tes la mais-tres- se,

coeur] vous es- tes

la mais-tres- se,] Car de son coeur vous es- tes la mais-tres- se.

la mais-tres- se,] vous es- tes la mais-tres- se._____

la mais-tres- se, [vous es- tes la mais-tres- se,] vous es- tes la mais-tres- se.

vous [es- tes la mais-tres- se.]_____

la mais-tres- se, vous [es- tes la mais-tres- se,] vous es- tes la mais-tres- se.

15. Si le souffrir donnoit espoir

16. Toutes les nuicts je ne pense qu'en celle

17. Le loyer de mon service

62

18. Si mon coeur a faict offence

fois, Ne [se doit pu- nir,] Ne se doit pu- nir deux fois, Ne [se doit pu-nir deux fois.]

Ne se doit, Ne [se doit pu-nir deux fois,] Ne se doit pu-nir _____ deux fois. _____

Ne [se doit pu-nir deux fois,] Ne se doit pu-nir, Ne se doit pu- nir deux fois. _____

Ne se doit pu- nir deux fois, Ne [se doit pu-nir deux fois,] Ne se doit pu- nir deux fois.

_ pu-nir, Ne se doit pu- nir deux fois, Ne se doit _____ pu- nir deux fois.

19. Triste fortune au bas m'a voulu attirer

Superius

Tri- ste for- tu- ne, [Tri- -ste for- tu- ne] _____

Contratenor

Tri- ste for-tu- ne, _____ [Tri- ste for-

Quinta

Tri- ste for-tu- ne, [Tri- ste for-tu-

Tenor

Tri- ste for-tu- ne, [Tri- ste for-tu- ne] au

Bassus

Tri- ste for- tu- ne

66

20. Lucrec' un jour par force violée

21. O coeur hautain, o courage pudique

22. Tant seulement ton amour je demande

78

23. Puisqu'amour m'a voulu arrester

24. Si le Rubis par sa naive bonté

25. Chanson va-ten où je t'addresse

26. Contente vous d'avoir tel serviteur

27. Tout ce qui est au monde

28. De moins que Rien

DATE DUE

DEMCO 38-297